YOUR SONNET FOR THE DAY

Pratibha James

Clever Fox
PUBLISHING

Chennai • Bangalore

CLEVER FOX PUBLISHING
Chennai, India

Published by CLEVER FOX PUBLISHING 2022

ISBN: 978-93-56480-78-0

CONTENTS

CHILDHOOD

Of all the ages that one can be,
Of all the stages that happen to be,
One stands out prominently for me,
Childhood - pure, simple – as ever can be.

It's personified, not by innocence alone,
It's the time when responsibilities one doesn't
own.
It's life's foundation, the strong backbone,
To roam, be known and one's talents to hone.

Youth, middle age and senior years will come,
Life's challenges and trials should not make
one numb,
Victories, prayers, gratitude won't let one
succumb,
There's so much to experience, to prevent the
humdrum.

Time passes by and the present pushes one
further,
Memories from your childhood are there to
nurture.

SILENCE

There is a state, to experience is rare,
In this age of racing, from here to there.
Where is the here, what is the there?
Between them find it, with no compare.

The state of Silence – so subtle and serene,
Takes you inward, from the outward scene.
Into the warm depths of your soul so pristine,
From here spiritual strength, you can easily
glean.

Course yourself out from the sounds so vast,
To the present moment, from the Future and
Past.
To the here and now, your thoughts do cast,
Be all alone, experience the contrast.

When you shift your attention to the calm
world of Silence,
With peace, love, joy and contentment, you
make an Alliance.

THE CRUSH

He must have been 18 when he first saw her,
A face to remember, cannot forget her.
She was his classmate's younger sister,
Thus, out of bounds, a girl to remember.

They lived nearby, so they were neighbours,
He used to visit, to gain her favours,
But never once did he get to meet her,
Did she even know, of his Love's labour?

Alas! Life chose for them different directions,
Sure, his wife and offspring bring him
satisfaction,
Yet, she lingers gently taking his attention,
Oh, don't tell him, that this is transgression.

In moments of emptiness, his hearts
attachments he treasures,
And remind himself that memories are a big
source of pleasure.

YOUR PURPOSE AND WORTH

When you are a child, lost in your world, it never occurs to you,
The ups and downs, that parents feel, taking care of you.

Mum's voice and heartbeat, providing warmth, comfortable place to be,
Dad's arms and shoulders, provide protection, safest place to be.

School days are fun, with lots to learn, so much to touch and see,
College comes next, careers made, heart full of joy and glee.

You start to earn, and freedom is yours, no limits to time and space,
You've grown up now, you face the world, your finally in the race.

Your children are born, your pride and joy,
the apple of your eye,
They take your money, time and energy, all
that you signify.

You live for them, you sacrifice, you have to
help them grow,
You lead them on, and guide them too,
blessings on them bestow.

Then finally it dawns on you, the reason of
your birth,
The love and admiration in their eyes, that
reveals your worth.

THE OTHER GOD

You shall have no other Gods, you shall
worship me alone,
I, your God will watch over you, you will never
walk alone.
Despite the assurances and promises, written
by His finger on Stone,
We tend to lose faith, falling prey to doubt,
stop trusting on Him alone.

The other god we have placed our trust on, is
not visible to the eye,
Not made of spirit, flesh or earthly produce, us
it does crucify,
This god is present in our daily lives, our sins
to amplify,
Our actions betray how silently with it we
identify.

This god dwells deep within us, commonly
known by the name of Pride,
It makes us want to stand alone, above others,
causing great divide,
Looking down on others, brotherhood is lost,
in yourself your fortified,
The fruits of Love, joy, peace, hope, meekness
and gentleness are nullified.

Cast away your pride my friend, join hands,
aimlessly do not roam,
Never forget, that we are all here, simply to
walk each other home.

LIFE, DEATH & LIFE AGAIN

It's what we dread, it makes us sad, but it stares
at us most certain,
Breath shall cease, death shall come, we have to
draw the curtain.
Our race is run, our time is done, from sins
did we abstain?
Now take your soul, and walk up bold, to see
what you'll attain.

What we perceive, to be the end, is just another
station,
Some will get off, some will get on, it's not the
destination.
Hold on that thought, and linger on, feel that
deep sensation,
Let it pierce you, let it heal you, this process of
Mutation.

On one side fear, on one side love, between these we have lived,
There is no right, there is no wrong, do not you be deceived,
What is the good, what is the bad, from where were these derived?
Old body gone, your lessons learned, your new body has arrived.

Fear not this death, embrace it strong, stare at it, in its face,
Its hold is short, its grasp is weak, when you live your life with Grace.

TAKE A SPIN - EARTHLY JOURNEY

We build strong walls around us, to safeguard
our inner core,
From the dangers that lurk around us,
knocking on our hearts door.

We don't accept or trust the intentions of
fellow beings,
We doubt them and maintain distance with
them in our dealings.

Learn to stretch out your hand, believe that
trust begets trust,
Drop the veil you are hiding in, reveal yourself
to others you must.

All souls that come to this Earth, feel the same
joy and pain,
The spinning cycle of life equates us, when we
meet in this plane.

You cannot win or lose, in this journey as you involve,
Bear in mind you reason you came, is purely to evolve.

There is plenty to go around, so always give more than you take,
Collect not possessions, but loving memories you should make,
In acts of compassion, empathy and kindness you should partake,
Only then to the true purpose of life, your soul will remain awake.

BEAUTY OF THE GENDERS

As far as night is from day, as far as light is from dark,
The differences between them are often, highlighted as very stark.
Yet, to close this imaginary divide, with you I wish to embark,
Pray stay with me, and walk with me to understand my remark.

Surely the genders divide us, it's not just a matter of the physical,
We feel and think differently, covering also the emotional and mental,
Masculine control over feminine, all through history is despicable,
Feminine need for harmony, from the beginning is intrinsical.

Leaving the past behind us, we need to cherish
this difference,
Facing the future ahead of us, we need to
appreciate our experience,
Starting with trust and respect, on each other
we should take a chance,
Ending with patience and tolerance, together
we will find the balance.

We all belong to the same God, who made the
Heavens and Earth.
Displaying his image, likeness and Spirit, never
ye forget your worth.

THE POWER OF CHOICE

The state of feeling powerless, being trapped,
not in control,
The state of feeling vulnerable, unprotected
and exposed.
The intense fear that grips one, being not in
safety enclosed.
No one will move you out of this, please get
yourself composed.

Close your eyes for a moment, from the powers
pulling you outward,
Open your heart for a moment, to the powers
lying dormant inward.
This is the power of choice, with which
humans have been honoured,
Use this power of choice, invoke the energy
within you treasured.

There is a Fire deep within you, that for long
you have ignored,
The Water of fear has doused it, left it damp
and very cold.

Use the Air of courage to fan it, and watch the
flames glow,
Walk the Earth with confidence, the Universe
will help you soar.

Within each breath you can taste it, you need
to speak your voice,
Within each moment you can sense it , you
need to make that Choice.

SOULMATES

Whenever one talks of Soulmates, one tends to
think of romantic,
This places discriminatory limits, on relations
that are platonic.
All life is submerged in relationships, giving it
a touch of dramatic,
Alone - nothing can one accomplish, Here lies
the secret to magic.

Most relationships are not amorous, arising
purely out of our need,
Childhood passing to senescence, we are
guided along by our creed.
This journey lasts more than a lifetime, don't
try to gain on speed,
You're here to discover your prime, let
goodwill steer your deed.

Relationships offer you experience, that assist
your soul to sprout,
Stay aware and learn what it teaches, to
diversity of lessons be devout.
Children, parents, siblings, spouses, on
relations there is no limit,
Trusted friends or nasty neighbours, into life
pour in more Spirit.

As you go searching for your soulmate, nobody
should you leave out,
Every soul you meet is a soulmate, beauty
within you to help bring out.

FEMININITY

Cannot be contained in a definition,
Too abstract for an artist's rendition,
Not to be taken as an acquisition,
Having broken free from tradition.

Cannot be confined within a picture,
Too wild to be bound by scripture.
Not to be treated as a mere fixture,
Having capacity to create new structure.

Cannot be cowered by sheer aggression,
Too prudent to dismiss one's discretion,
Not to be tarnished by male reputation,
Having tenacity to contradict humiliation.

Femininity is an attribute too awe inspiring for
comprehension,
Full of courage and determination, all
sprinkled with affection.

THE MEANINGLESS CHASE

The Corporate world is mighty, power plays
and money rules.
Glass and concrete towers glisten brightly, this
endless race has made us mules.
Once you enter it holds you tightly, attracting
you with fancy tools.
Day by day you labour endlessly, searching for
desperate interludes.

Timelines are tight and stakes are high,
surrounded by strong competition,
You're all alone, you have no ally, this race is
ruled by fierce ambition.
Speed up, keep up else you die, or drown your
soul to keep position,
Company profit you must magnify, to your
own life causing attrition.

Nature gave humans a lot of blessings, but it
left out money and time,
Both of these we humans are chasing, running
after the illusive dime.
Stop with all this mindless racing, take control
while still in your prime,
Follow your souls gentle calling, return to
nature most sublime.

Surely one day, the futility of this chase will
sink deep inside of you,
For humanity's sake I pray it happens long
before its time for Adieu.

WHAT ARE THEY ASKING FOR

When you come across a beggar, what is it that you sense?
You sense?
Is it pride at your achievements, you live at your own expense.
Is it anger at those people, that society should them dispense.
You cannot deny that seeing them, puts you on the defence.

Each one of them has a story, surely not as happy as your own,
They don't have any family, on the streets they are thrown,
Surviving on kindness and mercy, of people to them unknown,
When they die will there be anyone, their absence to bemoan?

What is it that they are asking for - food,
shelter and clothes.
We can easily part with things like these, I will
dare to suppose.
Look beyond these needs to something lasting,
I do propose.
Walk with them on this journey, within dignity
do them enclose.

Training, Skills, Vocations, opportunity to
earn their daily bread,
Showered with your trust and respect, will take
them miles ahead.

THESE PRECIOUS SOULS

The animal kingdom is enriched with colours, sounds and beauty,
Embellished with feathers, fur or fins, they are a living bounty,
Each species distinct, unique, varying from the feisty to the dainty,
The Earth is their habitat, where they display nature's majesty.

They live and die and breathe like us, they have sensitivities,
They eat and sleep and play like us, they have personalities,
They feel and love and fear like us, they have their families,
To think that humans can exploit them, is a selfish fallacy.

This earth is theirs as much as ours, they wish to live in harmony,

We need to keep our wants aside to help
maintain the ecology,
We have taken them for granted, showing them
no sympathy,
We have used, abused, killed and skinned
them, very heartlessly.

In this journey of life, they are our fellow
souls, please see the affinity
You need to cherish them and nurture them,
please show your humanity.

FILLING THE VOID WITHIN

Living each day from dusk to dawn, running
from home to work,
The workload never seems to end, one is racing
around in a cirque,
Caring for one's near and dear, these
responsibilities one will not shirk,
Motivated by love for family, the long hours do
not seem to irk.

The days go by and turn to months, and
months turn into years,
The work starts getting monotonous, middle
age causing new fears,
The children flying away from the nest,
loneliness brings on tears,
It's a different phase of living now, a season
with new frontiers.

Life is far from over, but now one question's
the meaning of this race,
Was it for money or for power, what is it that
now we do embrace,
You need to search within yourself, this
question you must face,
What's done is done, and time is past, your
actions you cant erase.

This is the perfect time to add joyful
adventure, to this your precious journey,
Live for yourself, embrace your dreams, live
them, the days are not many.

JUST A LITTLE CONSIDERATION

It doesn't cost much to make a difference, just
a bit of consideration,
It doesn't cost all your time or money, just a
bit of kind attention.

A simple smile for someone you do not know,
A nod of acknowledgement, for someone you
do know.
A word of appreciation for a job well done.
A word of encouragement, when it's not well
done.
A helping hand, when there is work to be
done,

A pat on the back, when the work is all done.
A high five for celebration, when someone
achieves,
A hug giving confidence, when someone fails,
A listening ear, when someone needs to talk,
A silent presence, when someone needs to
think.

These simple acts can go a long way, go find something for any situation,
These gentle gestures have so much to say, you can be someone's inspiration.

BEYOND PERFECTION

We are obsessed with creating the flawless, of
going beyond the expected norm,
We are striving to refine excellence, outdoing
all barriers and trying to reform,
Staying within boundaries is unacceptable, it is
not considered wise to try to conform,
In the existing we do not find refinement, the
human limits we wish to transform,

All this striving for a better future, makes us
forget to live in the present.
All this chasing after some happiness, fills us
with a feeling of discontent,
All this pushing to meet tight timelines, makes
us wonder where time is spent,
All this competing against one another, will
bring to relationships great torment.

Instead of all the striving, live in the present
and savour each moment,

Instead of all the chasing, try to make someone
else's life more vibrant,
Instead of all the pushing, spend time on
things that are relevant.
Instead of all the competing, in your dealings
with others be clement.

You won't find perfection in power, money,
technology or physical attractions,
You'll find it in the hearts of humble people,
seen in their intent, words and actions.

CIRCUMSTANCES

Life places us in various situations and
circumstances,
We go through these either assured or taking
chances,
Either smiling or seeking help with desperate
glances,
Thus, revealing the colours of our individual
nuances.

If there were no changes and life remained
constant,
We would not be compelled to respond or
react,
Responding helps us grow and misfortunes
prevent
Reacting could awaken within you the tyrant.

People are intrinsically neutral, neither good
nor bad,
Circumstances they are put in, make them
happy and glad,

Handling the situation shows if they are
normal or mad,
With maturity and understanding are they
internally clad.

The temptation to judge another, you always
must eschew,
Put yourself in their circumstances, then ask
what would you do.

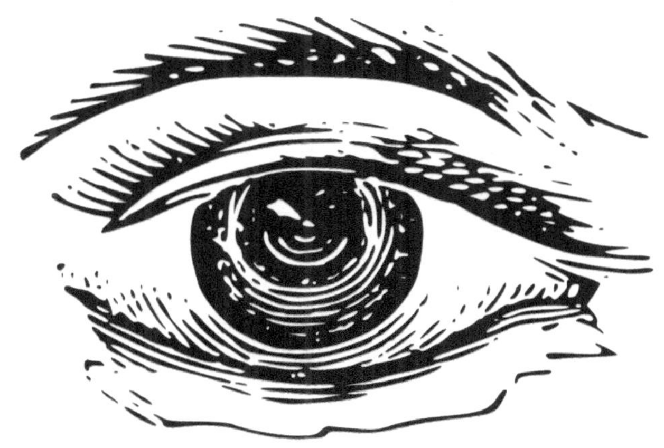

LOOKING BEYOND BELIEFS

Our religious beliefs teach us a great deal,
What to live by and how in prayer to kneel,
Showing what to value and what is the real,
Living each day lovingly with gratitude and zeal.

Belief of one religion may not match with another,
In essence alike, but in interpretation they differ,
Put those aside, with them don't ever you bother,
Focus on the essence, help to bring all together.

Those values are pure with a coverage universal,
Reducing all diversity, and creating no rival,
Tolerance, appreciation and winning approval,
For the existence of humanity, this is pivotal.

Delve deep in the religious beliefs to see what lies beyond,
The beauty and purpose of your life is far more profound.

MUSIC

The artful interplay between
sound and silence,
Of beats playing in a rhythmic
sequence.
Melodies flowing in a graceful
cadence,
Notes forming a wordless sentence.

Music is a universal language,
Waves of sound relaying a message,
Raw emotions it can assuage,
In hearts inspire great courage.

Music holds within it the power to heal,
Carrying vibrations by nature genteel,
Brings out emotions, you may try to conceal,
Your inner sacred being, encourage you to
feel.

If music can move you, consider yourself
fortunate,
Heavens energy within you is beginning to
resonate.

PRAYER

It is the state of seeking without asking,
It is the state of waiting without expecting,
It is the state of listening without talking,
It is you connecting with your higher self.

It is the state of accepting without
complaining,
It is the state of trusting without controlling,
It is the state of walking without seeing,
It is you connecting with the Universe.

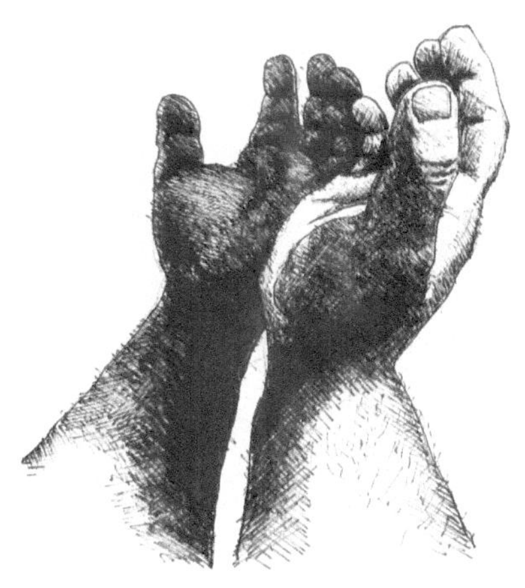

It is the delving within yourself rather than the
outside,
It is the harnessing of your energy and
potential inside,
It is the abandoning of self-pity, then your life
preside,
It is the facing of challenges, then taking
control to decide,
It is the staring hard at fear and to yourself
courage provide,

Because answers to all your prayers, actually
only within you do reside.

THE GURU

The Guru is the one who dispels the darkness
of ignorance,
Not the one who from your life will remove
hinderance,
Not the one to whom you run to with your
life's grievance,
Not the one who will teach you to go seek
vengeance.

The Guru is the one who from afar can provide
guidance,
Your role extends beyond merely paying him
obeisance,
Your role includes facing your karma with
endurance,
Your role is to do your duty placing him in
your reliance.

The Guru is the one who never forces from
you, obedience,
Removes ignorance and encourages you to live
with confidence,
Provides guidance as your human experience
you need to enhance,
Connect with your higher self, and with other
souls seek consonance.

The Guru will only throw light for you, on the
path you need to walk,
Your strength and trust will carry you, so your
potential you will unlock.

LURE OF COUNTRY LIFE

Living your life in the bright neon lights of the city,
The fast pace, the busy life, bursting full of suavity,
Looking for power, adulation, fame and opportunity,
The race to quickly reach sophistication and prosperity.

This long arduous journey creates within a deep cavity,
For the calm rustic charm, which in the city is a rarity,
Bringing the realization that this is just worship of vanity,
A profound longing for time to stand still, becomes priority,

Leave behind the concrete jungle, this life of complexity,
For the stillness of the villages, where noise is in paucity,

For the fresh air and pure smells, you can
breathe to capacity,
For the peace of the simple life, you can find
here your sanity.

With cosmos and nature, we need to secure our
identity,
In it anchor and stay connected to help save
our humanity.

FUTILITY OF WAR

Crime is unforgiveable and organised crime
even more,
On a larger scale with evil intent, for society it
is a sore,
Too violent and destructive, not anymore can
we ignore,
War is simply organised crime on humanity at
its very core.

We teach our children about wars in
humanity's history,
Praising one side for their tact, bravery and
victory,
Often adding exaggerated stories of pride and
glory,
Erasing the innocent victims of this carnage
from memory.

Wars mean that our leaders lack the ability to
communicate,
Brotherhood and unity, such attributes they
need to advocate.

On cooperation, not competition, our actions
we should predicate.
Survival of all, not just the fittest, this is what
we should inculcate.

From history we should learn, our mistakes not
to replicate,
If peace we can't practice, ourselves we will
eradicate.

MARRIAGE

We all have our reasons for entering into
marriage,
It could be love, looks, money or
companionship.
Starting with celebration, it's a gift-wrapped
bondage,
Keep going back in time, to the days of your
courtship.

This seems less a partnership, more like a
right-of-passage,
Where although you win, you have to give up
self-ownership.
Growing older and wiser together, is what we
always envisage,
Facing together the vicissitude of life, we
develop a unique kinship,

Marriage has within it for you an unexpectant advantage,
An honest critic by your side, who will not always you worship.
Reveal your weak areas, and to change them will encourage,
Making the marriage a spiritually benefiting relationship.

Whatever be your reason for entering into marriage,
It will never be easy, but will provide your soul leverage.

IT WON'T HAPPEN TO ME

When we are inexperienced and young, we are
full of innocence,
We are trusting, positive and completely
believe in our competence,
That nothing can ever stop us, and
interruptions will keep a distance,
Misfortunes happen to others, but in our life
they show an absence.

Along with the good and happy times,
challenges will surely follow us,
We tend to dread and fear them, and consider
them very ominous,
Fearing the worst, we lose courage, making
ourselves anxious,
Forgetting that our soul, was actually searching
for this very impetus.

Life is full of surprises, be always prepared for
the unexpected.
Accepting whatever comes, we can go through
it undaunted.

The unexpected makes you lonely, but know your not isolated,
You'll surely find many on your path, try to stay connected.

Trust in your inner strength, face the unpleasant without deterrence,
Faithfully standing by you, will be the uplifting hand of providence.

RAISING OUR SONS

We understand the need to raise our daughter
like we do our son,
Prepare her to be self-reliant and take on the
baton.
To create a position of strength and an identity
of her own.
Ability to think for herself, not be judged by
society's opinion.

We also need to raise our son like we do our
daughter,
To learn to be fluid and flexible like water,
To recognize the confidence in the ability to
surrender,
To experience the strength the ability to be
tender.

We can win more hearts with kindness, than
can be done with force,
Strength of mind is good for strategy, that of
heart for creating peace,

Angry words will cause you only harm, put
compassion in your voice,
Sharing builds true relationships, than you can
do by looking fierce.
As we teach our sons to be masculine, and have
a strong passionate side,

Also teach them to be feminine and embrace
their nurturing softer side.

CATS

Cats are very intriguing, in a quiet sort of way,
You'll see meaningful purpose, in their
graceful silent sway.
They are very good at listening, but don't have
much to say,
If you aren't really interesting, they will just
walk away.

You don't really choose a cat, they decide to
stay,
Nights are meant for hunting, sleep
throughout the day.
Never try to own a cat, your love they will
repay,
Look out for purrs and headbutts, and gifts of
their prey.

You cannot compare them to dogs, who always want to play.
A slow blink every now and then, lets you know things are okay,
They wander off occasionally, for their safety you should pray,
When they come back to your home, praise you should display.

Once you've been owned by a cat, you just cannot breakaway,
Their eyes and meows and memory, at your heart will always play.

MODERN DAY SLAVERY

It is far more rampant, than we are willing to
admit,
Displaying a vicious, and barbaric human trait,
That violently desecrates, the exquisite human
spirit,
Human trafficking and slavery, we should not
permit.

Children in their homes, with their parents
should inhabit,
Not be used as child soldiers, for political or
religious benefit,
Not be taught to use guns, in war zones end up
as puppets,
Their innocence all stolen, thru fear be made
to submit.

Enhancement of women, should be every
society's summit,
Not selling them in prostitution, for pleasure
or monetary profit,

Not be treated as a plaything, their mind and body exploit,
Their sanctity all defiled, their rich potential inhibit.

These were people like you and me, dumped into humanity's cesspit,
If we don't act to prevent this, we are guilty of being complicit.

MIRACLE

A miracle is not extraordinary, or even
remotely unnatural,
Rather it is the last step, of a process purely
rational,
A miracle isn't something, coming from the
external,
Emanated from within you, it's absolutely
internal.

It starts as a single thought, having in it
potential,
Its fuelled by your energy, from your heart
- emotional,
Its spurred on by desire, based on your dreams
– logical,
You are right at the point, where human meets
spiritual.

The thought grows bigger, taking on a form
pictorial,
You imagine in and feel it, to your being now
it is central,

The Universe will then support you, for obstacle removal.
Your thought materialises, you have achieved phenomenal.

You have to be your own god, break away from the traditional,
Manifesting your own miracle, for humans is surely natural.